FARTY MARTY

B. J. WARD

STEVEN KELLOGG

A PAULA WISEMAN BOOK
Simon & Schuster Books for Young Readers
NEW YORK LONDON TORONTO SYDNEY NEW DELHI

For my dearest Makena lei
—B. J. W.

Love to Kelly and Makena lei
—S. K.

SIMON & SCHUSTER BOOKS FOR YOUNG READERS
An imprint of Simon & Schuster Children's Publishing Division
1230 Avenue of the Americas, New York, New York 10020
Text copyright © 2013 by B. J. Ward • Illustrations copyright © 2013 by Steven Kellogg
SIMON & SCHUSTER BOOKS FOR YOUNG READERS is a trademark of Simon & Schuster, Inc.
For information about special discounts for bulk purchases, please contact
Simon & Schuster Special Sales at 1-866-506-1949 or business@simonandschuster.com.
The Simon & Schuster Speakers Bureau can bring authors to your live event. For more information or to book an event,
contact the Simon & Schuster Speakers Bureau at 1-866-248-3049 or visit our website at www.simonspeakers.com.
Book design by Chloë Foglia • The text for this book is set in Caslon and Odette.
The illustrations for this book are rendered in mixed water-based media.
Manufactured in China • 0813 SCP
2 4 6 8 10 9 7 5 3 1
Library of Congress Cataloging-in-Publication Data
Ward, B. J. (Betty Jean), 1944–
Farty Marty / B.J. Ward ; illustrated by Steven Kellogg. — 1st ed.
p. cm.
"A Paula Wiseman Book."
Summary: Although Mary Jane Lemon loves her cat Marty, others are offended by the sounds and smells
that come from his rear until Ms. Chen, a voice tutor, discovers that Marty's "audio output" is quite remarkable.
ISBN 978-1-4424-3901-6
ISBN 978-1-4424-3902-3 (eBook)
[1. Stories in rhyme. 2. Flatulence—Fiction. 3. Cats—Fiction. 4. Entertainers—Fiction.
5. Humorous stories.] I. Kellogg, Steven, ill. II. Title.
PZ8.3.W2124Far 2013
[E]—dc23
2012023597

Mary Jane Lemon loved her cat.

She proudly named him Marty.

But when he went to show-and-tell, Bud Baxter yelled,

It was true that strange sounds would pop out of his tush.

A tweet,

or a toot,

or a croak,

or a whoosh.

"Is this normal for cats?" Mrs. Blurgmeester wondered.
"It's a SKUNK, not a cat!" the school principal thundered.

The principal's note upset Mary Jane's granny.

Mary Jane wailed,

"I LOVE HIM!"

Marty purred from both ends.

Ms. Chen, a voice tutor,
arrived at their home.
"Today," she said brightly,
"we're writing a poem!
We'll recite it in French,
and then, for our snack,
I've brought French cheese and grapes
in this hand-painted sack."

They sat down to work . . . then they heard Marty gag.
He had eaten the grapes, the French cheese, and . . . the bag!

Then rising from Marty came a strange, haunting tune. "Why, that's unmistakably 'AU CLAIR DE LUNE'!" Ms. Chen cried, then added, "But how can this be? Your cat eats French cheese... and then plays Debussy?

To experiment further, they fed the cat pasta.
"*Te amo!*" crooned Marty.

Ms. Chen hollered,

"First French! Now Italian! This testing reveals,
Marty's audio output is inspired by his meals!"

The next day they learned of a gala pet show.

Ms. Chen had cooked hot dogs
and smothered the franks
in baked beans from Boston.
The cat purred his thanks.

Then he opened with fireworks,
stunning the crowd.

"IT VIOLATES CODE!"

If Marty was rattled,
it never once showed.

He inspired them to sing out,
with one rousing voice
that historical classic,
the country's first choice,
our national treat,
and our musical candy:

the jaunty,
jumping,
jolly chords
of "YANKEE DOODLE"

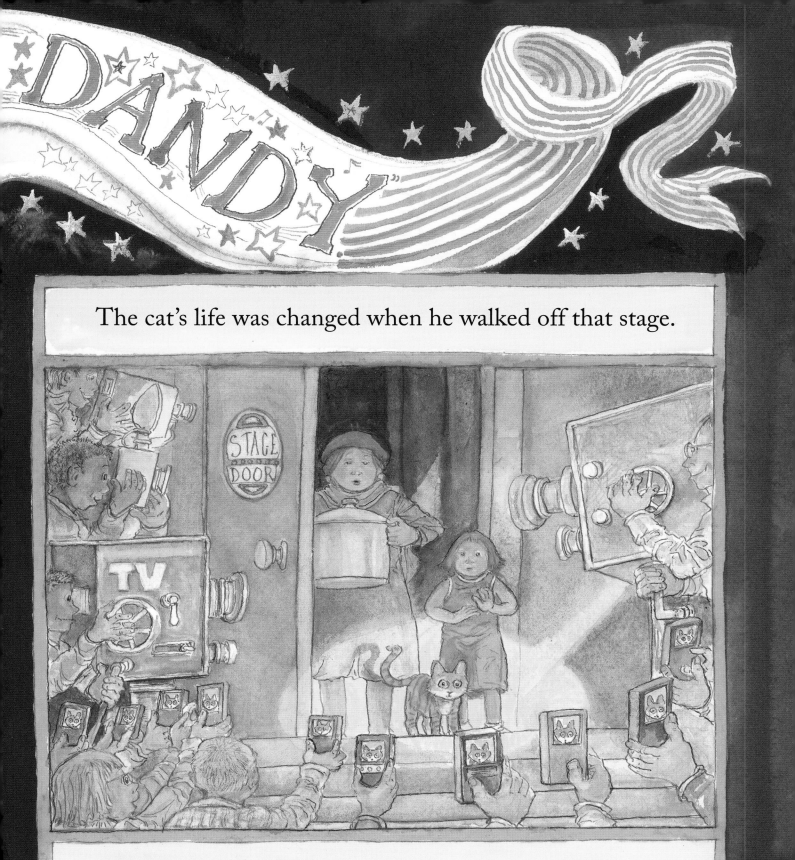

The cat's life was changed when he walked off that stage.

He had shot from class joke to the national rage.

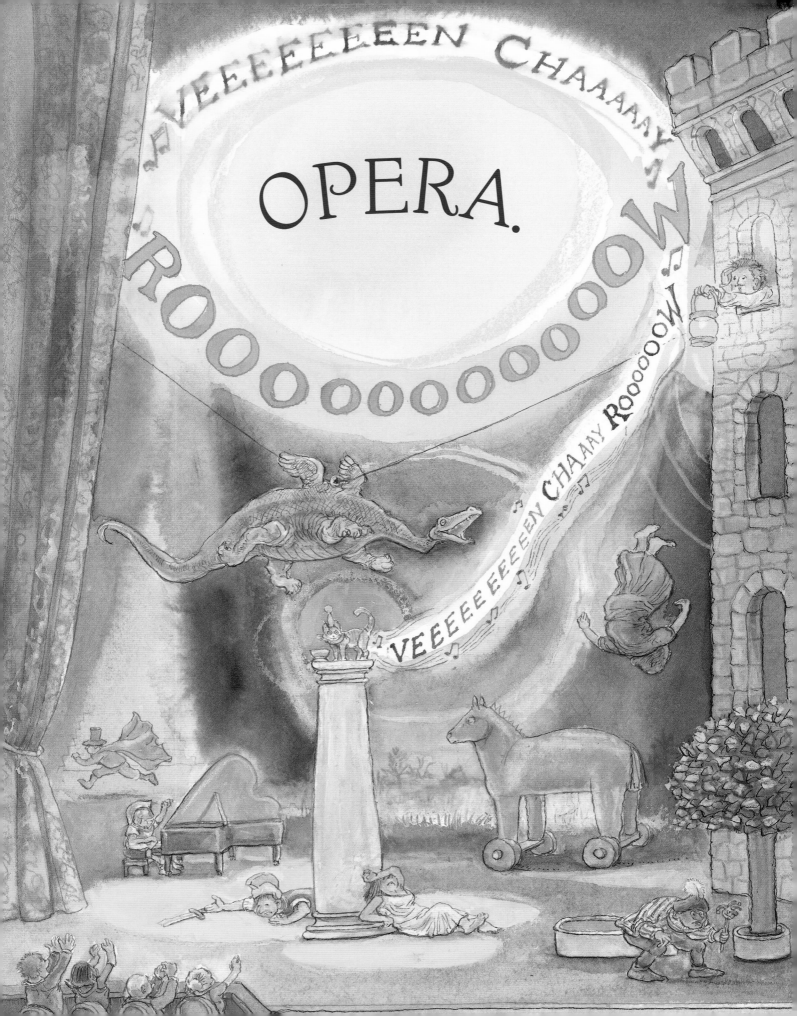

Even RAP was his thing!

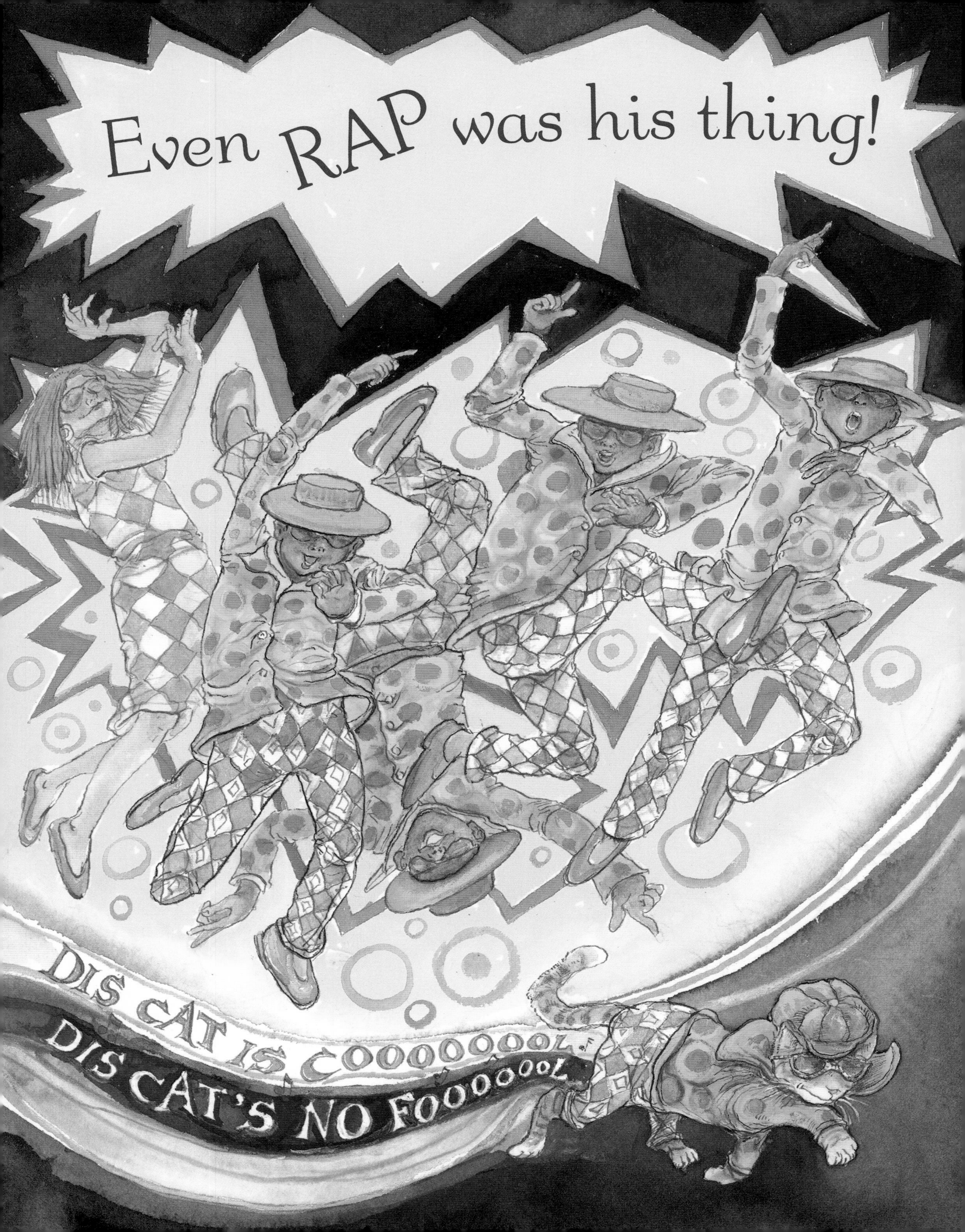

The rappers and roadies draped Marty in bling.

They voted him "Best Solo Artist in Punk."
And dubbed him "Dude Marty, da Cat Masta Skunk!"

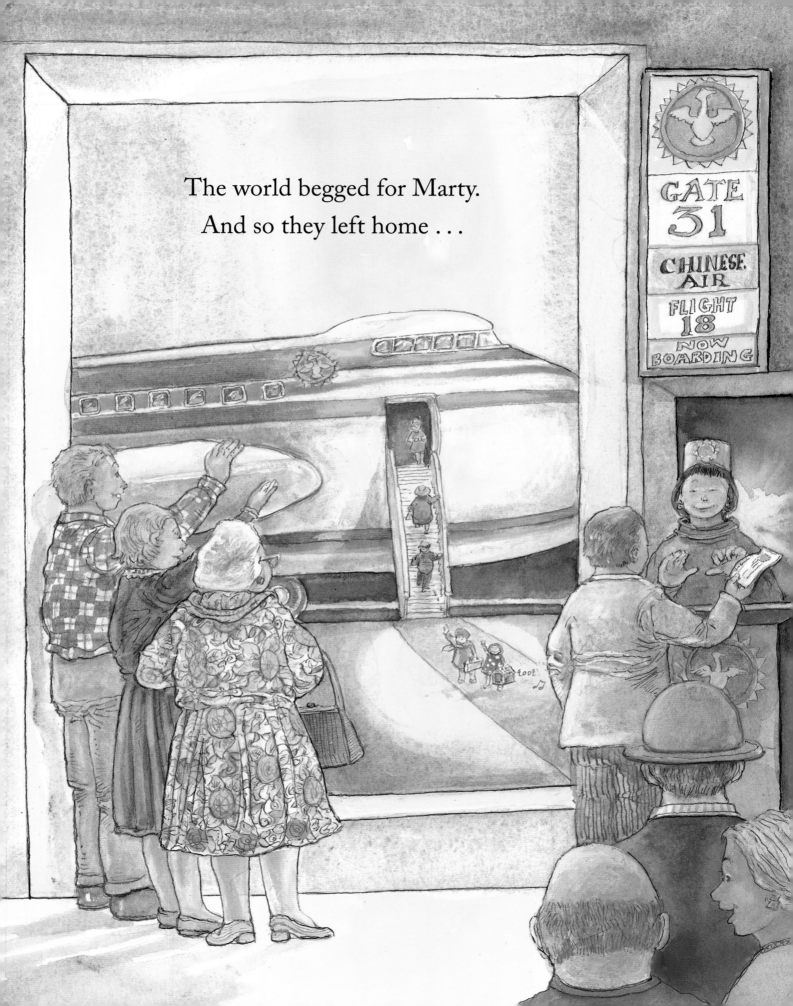

The world begged for Marty.
And so they left home . . .

. . . for China,

欢迎 欢迎 欢迎 欢迎 欢迎 欢迎 欢迎

Welcome to
☆ **DUDE MARTY** ☆
Da Cat Masta Skunk

地球上的和平 . . . 商普男人，女人和猫

MARTI

and Egypt,

السلام على الرضا والوفاء الا يافت مسنح يجمع الرجل والنساء والقطط

THE SPHINX
STINKS,
WE ♥ LOVE
MARTY!

REVIVE
CAT
WORSHIP

and
Rome.

In France the perfumers perfected the art
of bottling the cat's scent, which they labeled
La Farte.

At last the tour ended. The travelers came home.
"Mad About Marty" became their next poem.

Mary Jane wrote the verses,

Ms. Chen did the art.

Marty's story, when published, topped the bestseller chart.

Even Granny was thrilled by the family cat's fame.

And Mary Jane's principal changed the school's name.

MARTY LEMON ELEMENTARY SCHOOL

ODE TO
MARTY

But, though famous and rich,
Mary Jane said for her,
the best thing was still
Marty's sweet, loving purr.

So the next time you're watching TV with your pet,
and detect smells and noises . . .
please . . . don't be upset!

Be delighted
if you hear
a gurgle
or tweet.

You might have a gold mine asleep at your feet.